For Ruby Dew, our little rainbow

Noah's Bed copyright © Frances Lincoln Limited 2004
Text copyright © Jim Coplestone 2004
Illustrations copyright © Lis Coplestone 2004

First published in Great Britain in 2004 by
Frances Lincoln Children's Books, 4 Torriano Mews,
Torriano Avenue, London NW5 2RZ

www.franceslincoln.com

Distributed in the USA by Publishers Group West

British Library Cataloguing in Publication Data
available on request

ISBN 1-84507-002-X

Printed in China

1 3 5 7 9 8 6 4 2

Noah's Bed

Lis and Jim Coplestone

FRANCES LINCOLN CHILDREN'S BOOKS

Eber helped Grandpa Noah
and Grandma Nora to build a huge Ark,
to keep their family and a pair
of every kind of animal safe
when the big flood came.

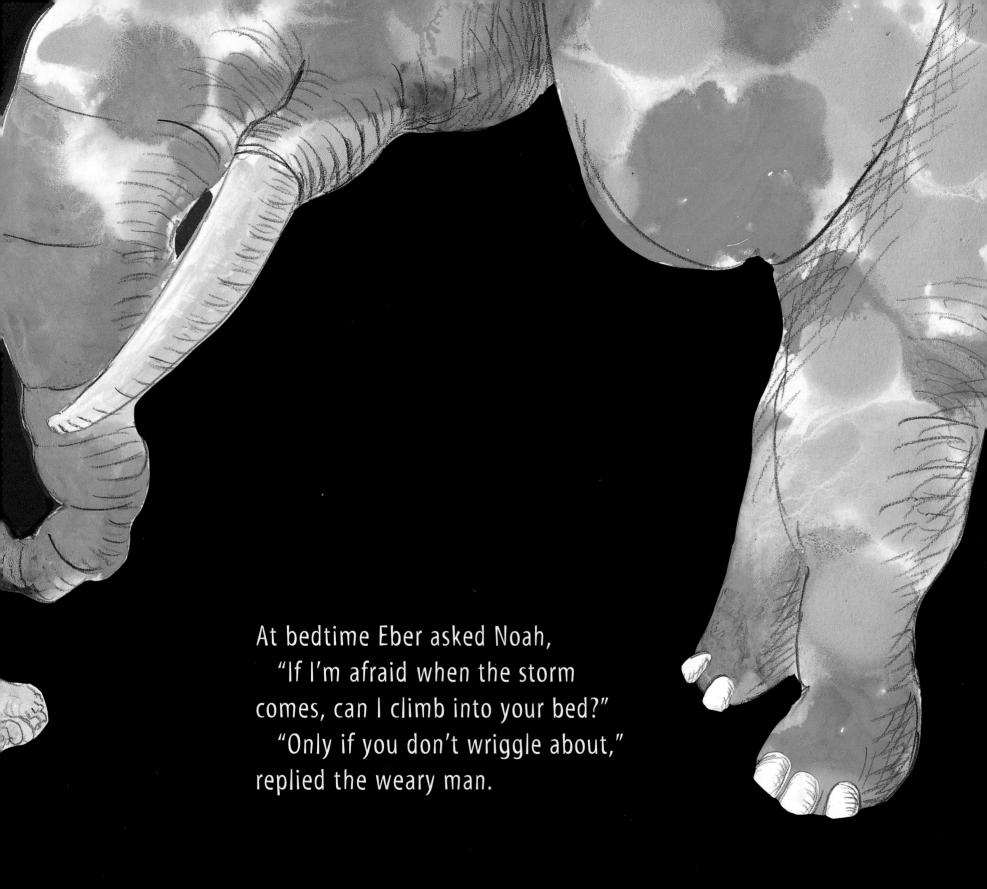

At bedtime Eber asked Noah,
  "If I'm afraid when the storm
comes, can I climb into your bed?"
  "Only if you don't wriggle about,"
replied the weary man.

The rain fell.
The water rose.
The Ark rocked like a giant cradle
and lulled Eber and all the animals to sleep.

"Good night every two," Noah whispered.

All was calm inside the Ark,
but outside the storm was gathering.
Wild winds stirred among the clouds.
The birds of paradise woke up in a terrible flap.

A bright forked tongue of lightning flickered.
The scaly green iguanas woke up and shivered with fear.

The wind howled around the Ark
and woke the lions.
They twitched in alarm
from their neat whiskers
to their straggly tail-tips.

Thunder stampeded across the sky.
Even the hefty elephants were frightened
by that fearful earful.

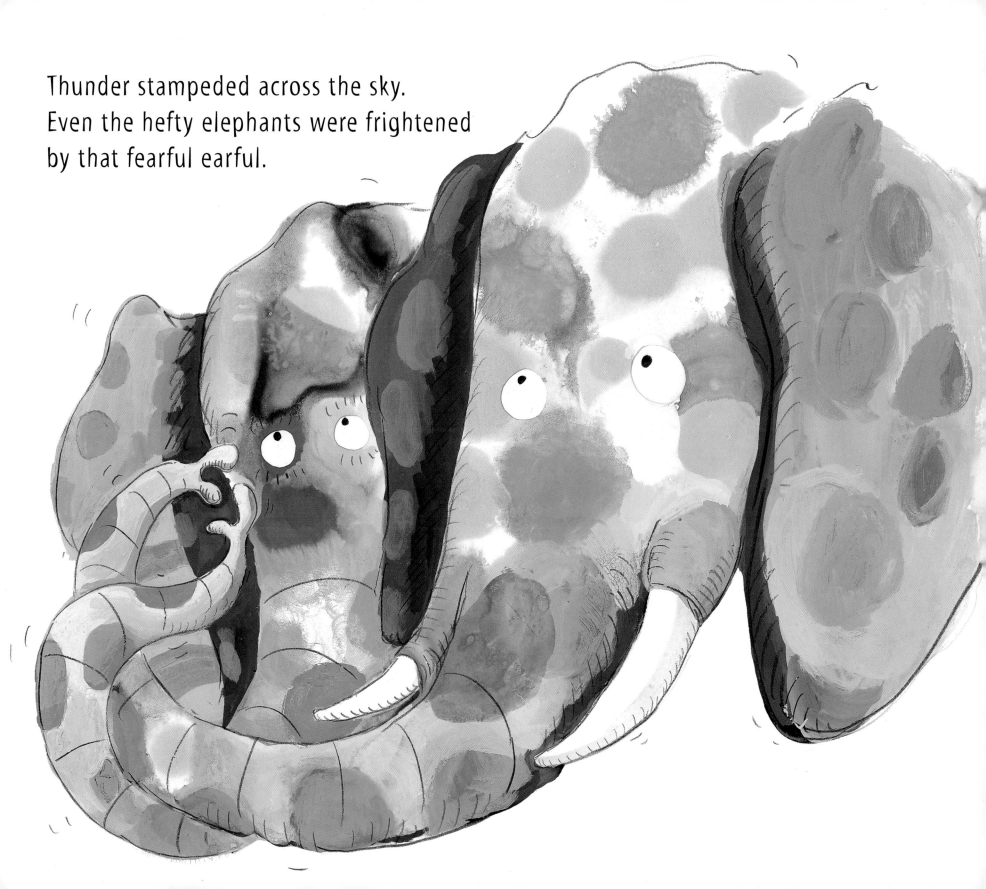

A gigantic CRACK of thunder
made Eber sit up.
In a flash, he was creeping through
the dark Ark, to his grandparents' bed.

"Cuddle me up, Grandpa, I'm scared!"
the little boy mumbled into Noah's huge beard.
    "All right, but remember, no wriggling!" whispered Noah.
    Eber and his grandparents snuggled down
to sleep again and all was peaceful aboard the Ark.

But then...

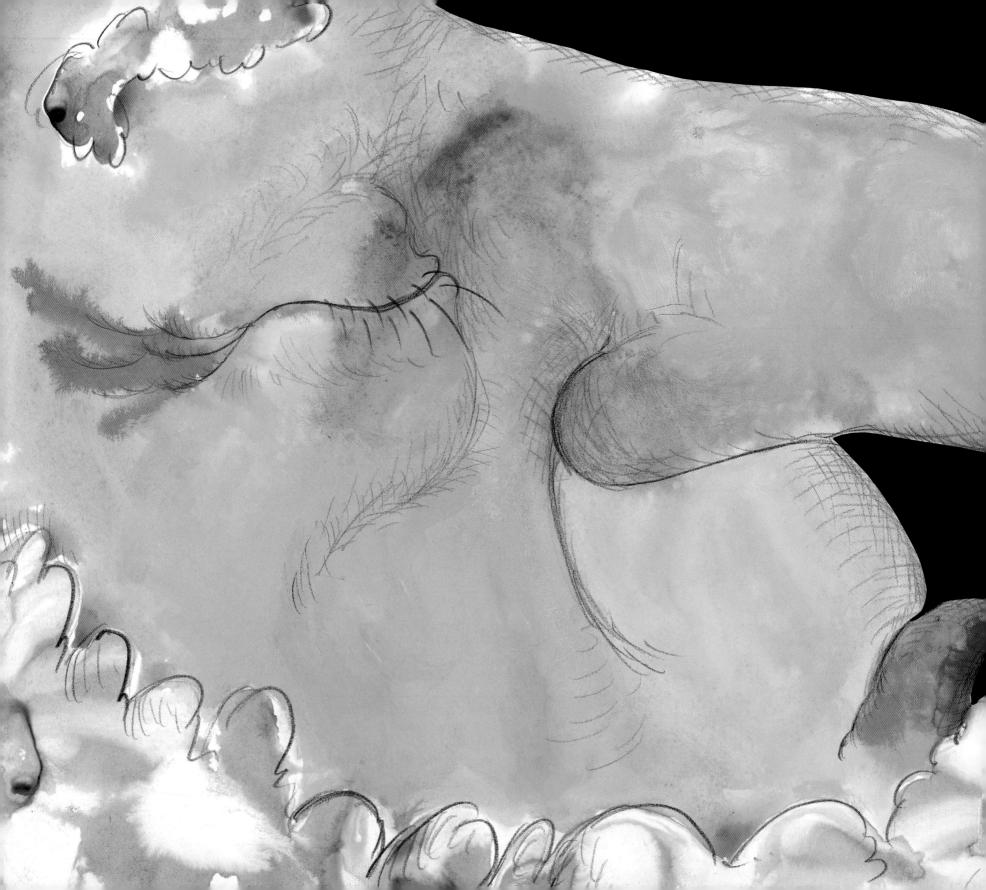

something tickled Noah's nose.
   "Aawfff," he grumbled.
"Your hair is tickly, Eber.
Please stop fidgeting and go to sleep."

But then...

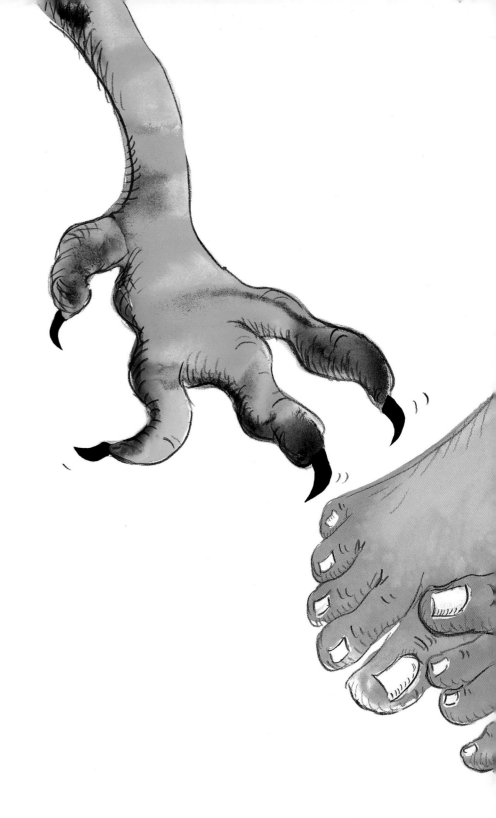

something scratched Nora's leg.
"Aaaagh!" she squawked.
"I must cut your toenails, Eber.
Do try to keep still, dear."

But then...

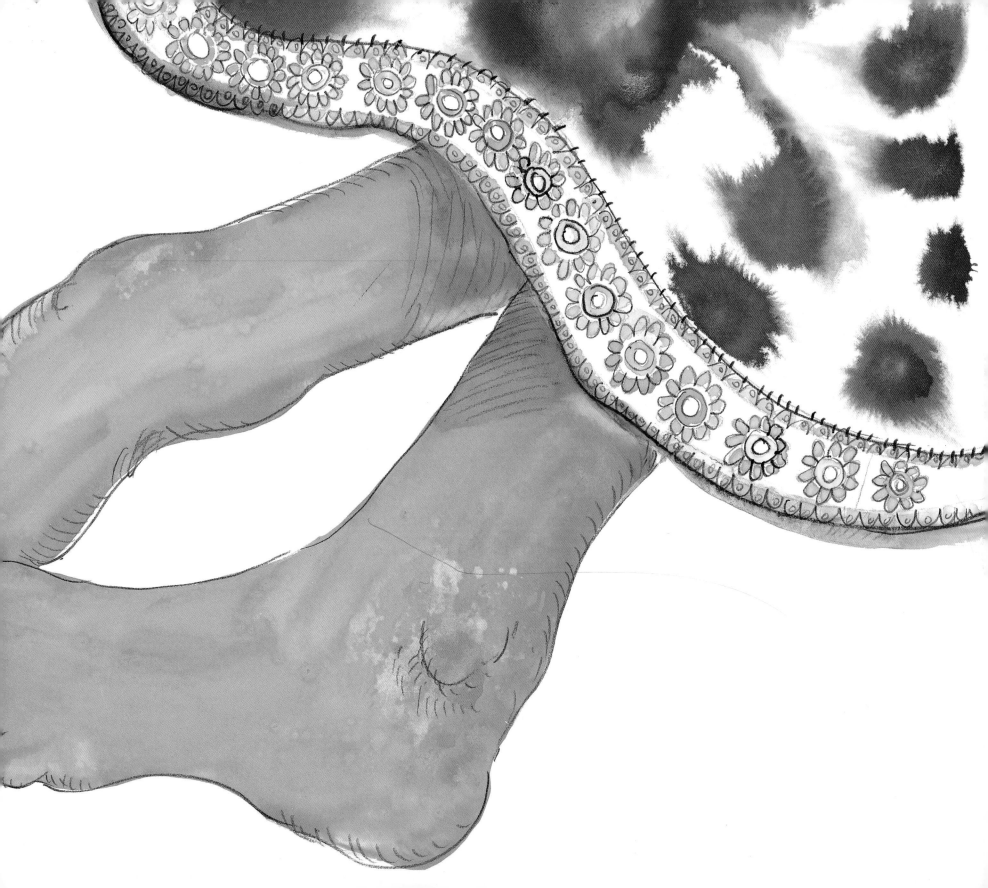

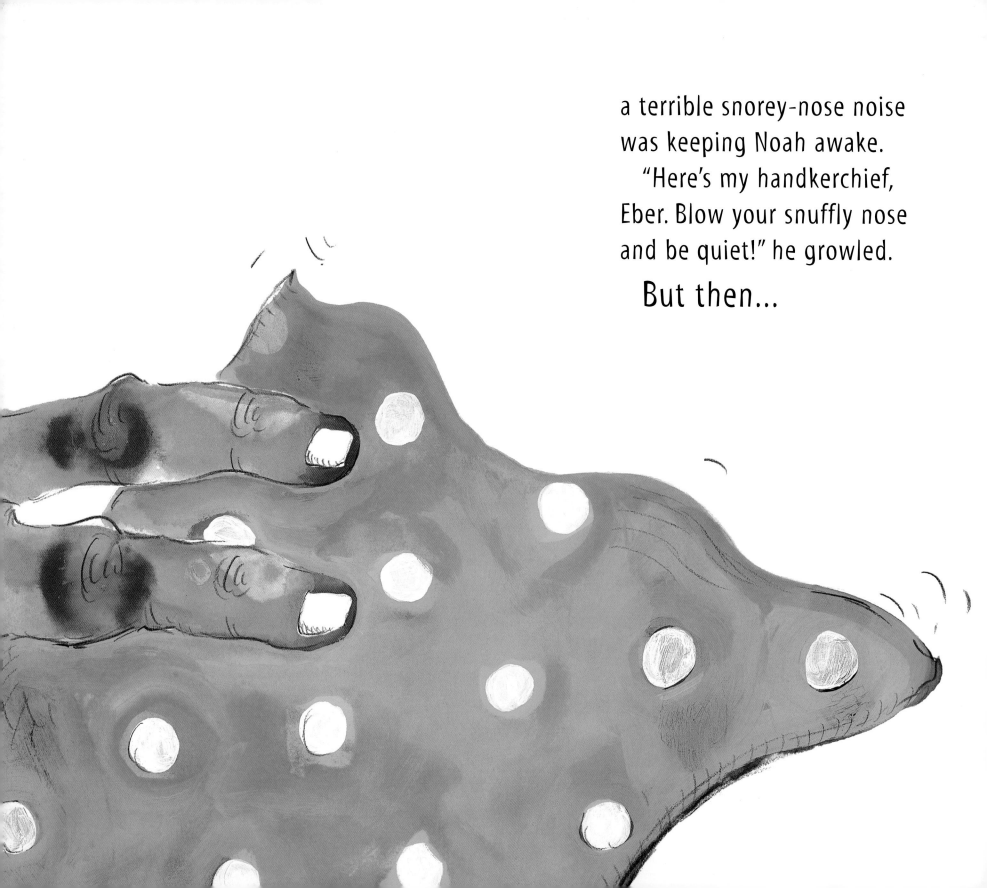

a terrible snorey-nose noise
was keeping Noah awake.
"Here's my handkerchief,
Eber. Blow your snuffly nose
and be quiet!" he growled.

But then...

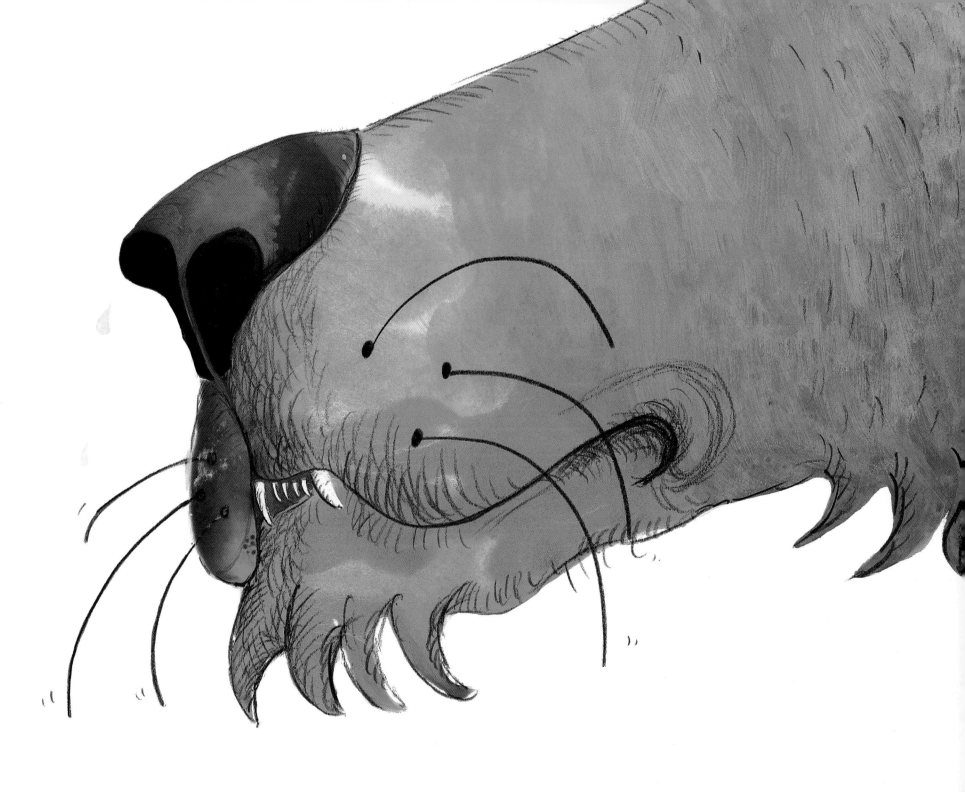

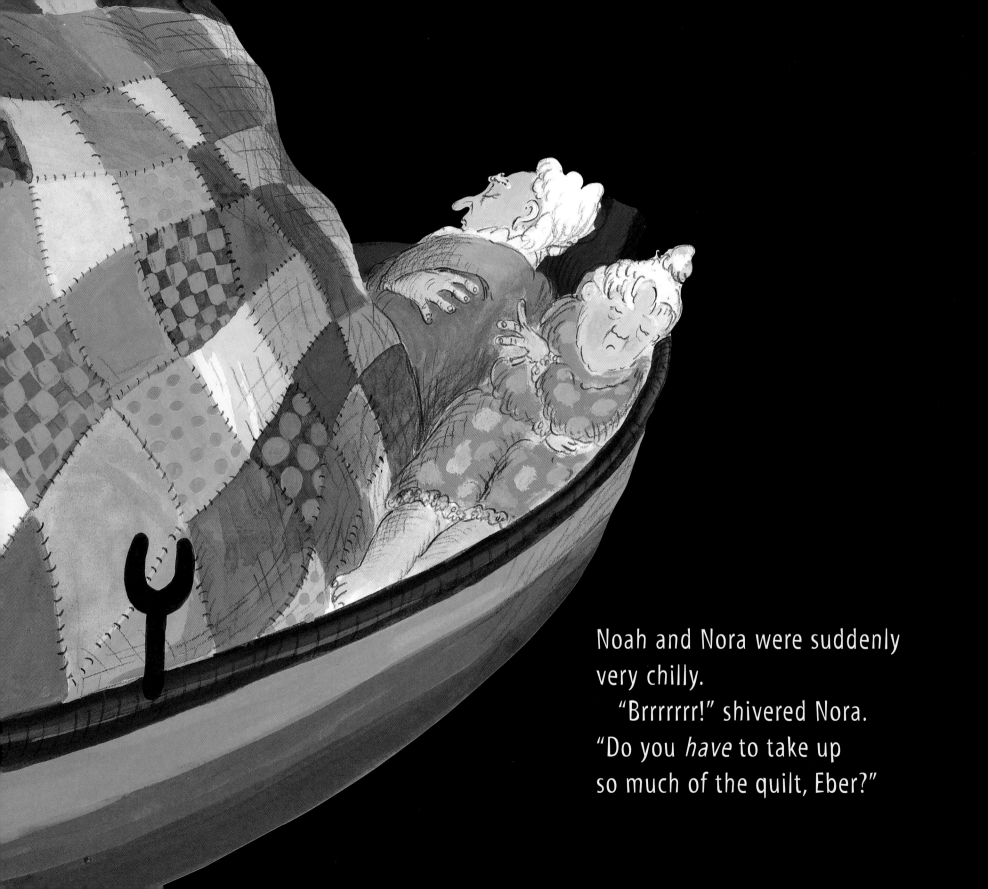

Noah and Nora were suddenly
very chilly.
  "Brrrrrrr!" shivered Nora.
"Do you *have* to take up
so much of the quilt, Eber?"

But for poor Noah it was the last straw.
"RIGHT, THAT'S ENOUGH, EBER.
BACK TO YOUR OWN BED YOU GO!"

He struck a match and lit the lamp...

and there in the bed were…

two tickly birds of paradise,
two scratchy green iguanas,
two snorey-nose lions,
two hefty elephants…

and Eber who was fast asleep.

Animals Brag About Their Bottoms

MAKI SAITO

Translated by Brian Bergstrom

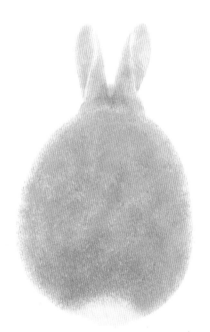

Look at my bottom!

GREYSTONE KIDS

GREYSTONE BOOKS • VANCOUVER / BERKELEY

My bottom is such a round bottom—
and so cute, don't you think?

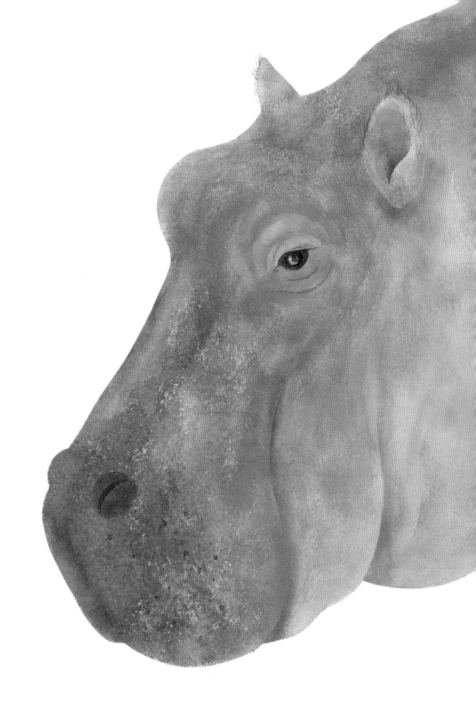

I have a round bottom too.
So round—and so-o-o big!

Just look!

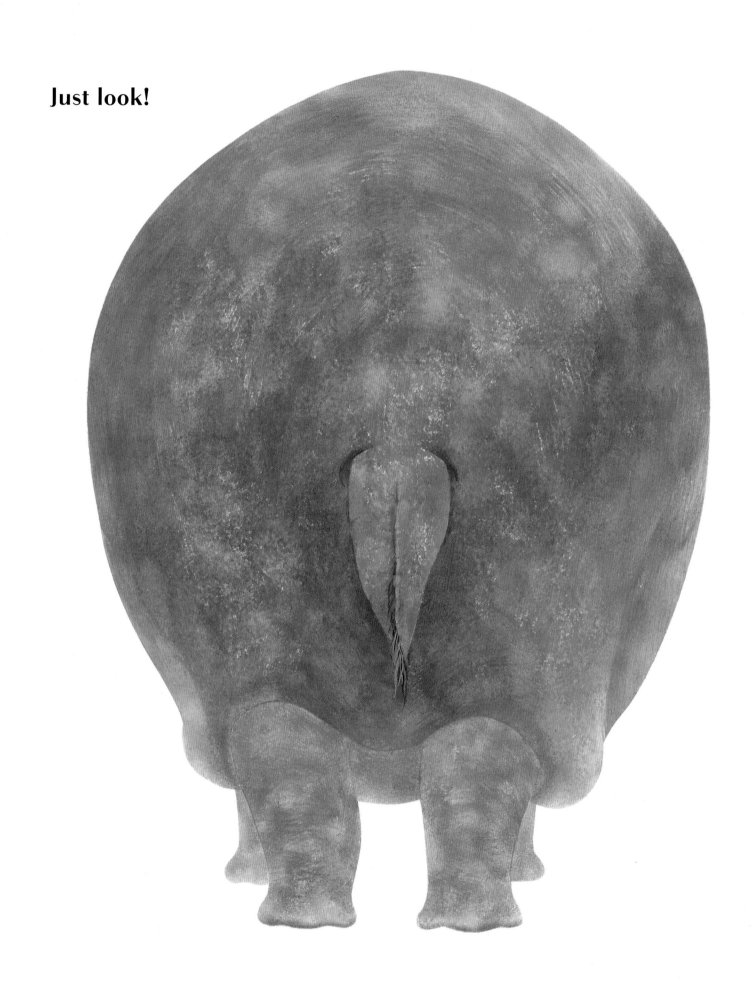

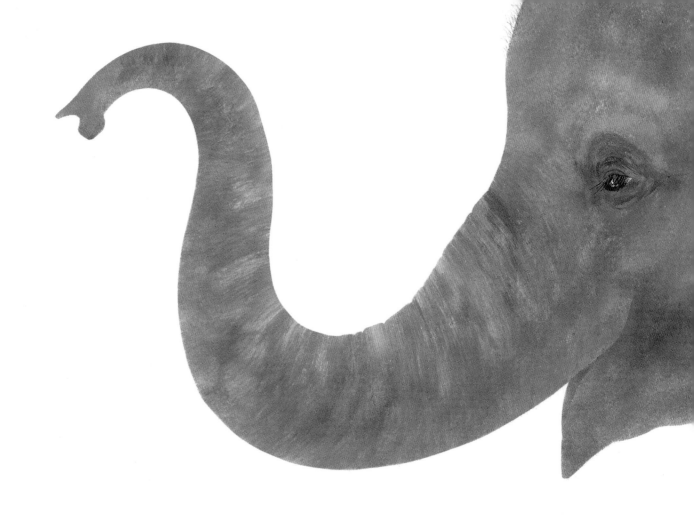

My bottom's even bigger.
So much bigger!

Look how big!

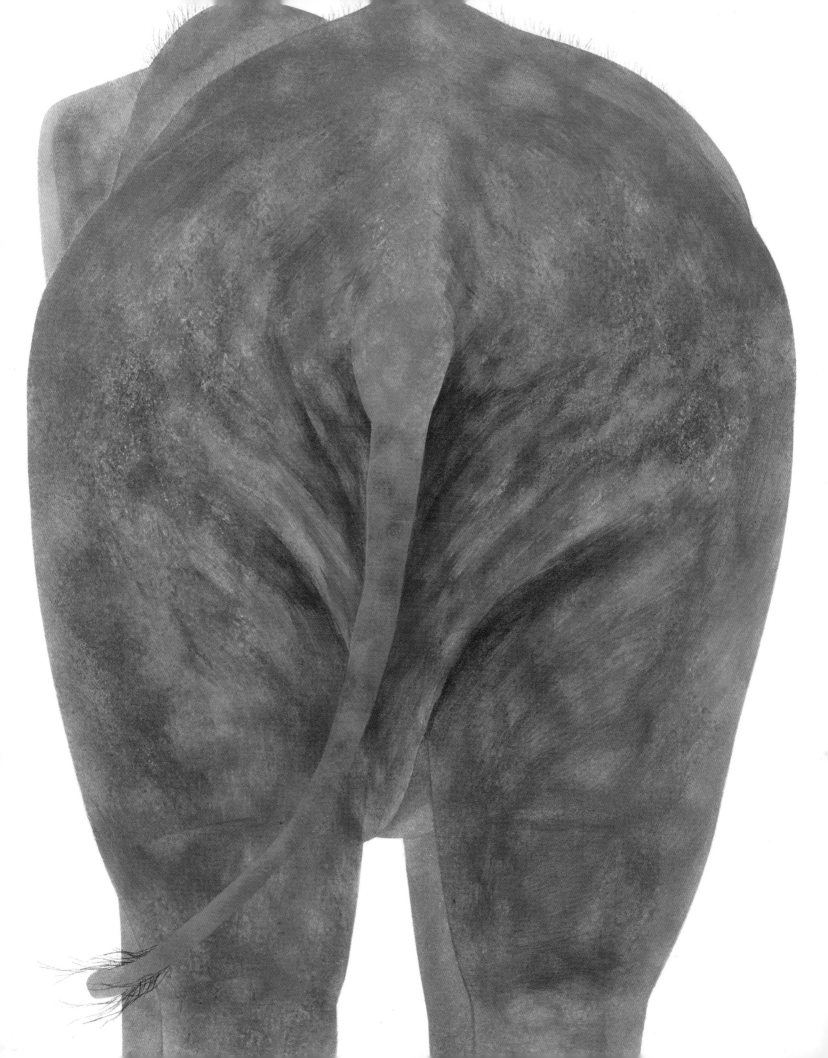

Look at our bottoms! They're covered in stripes.

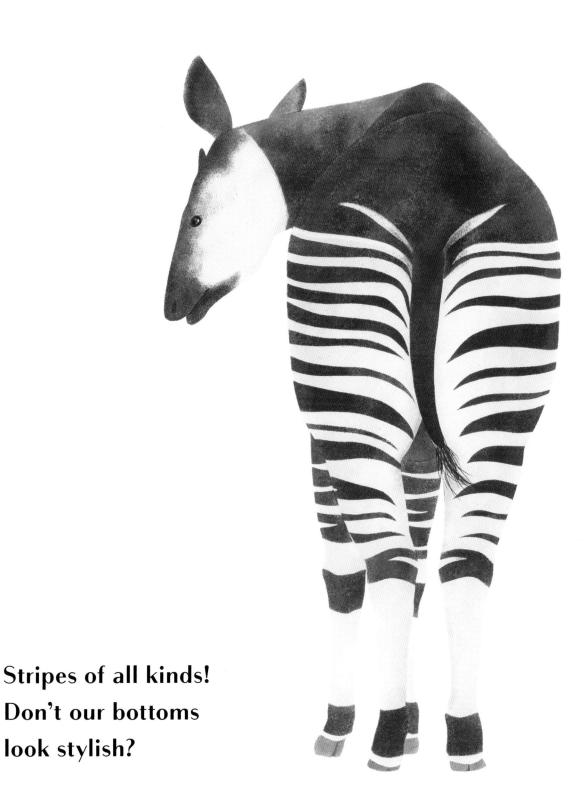

**Stripes of all kinds!
Don't our bottoms
look stylish?**

What about my bottom?
Is it patterned like the rest of me?

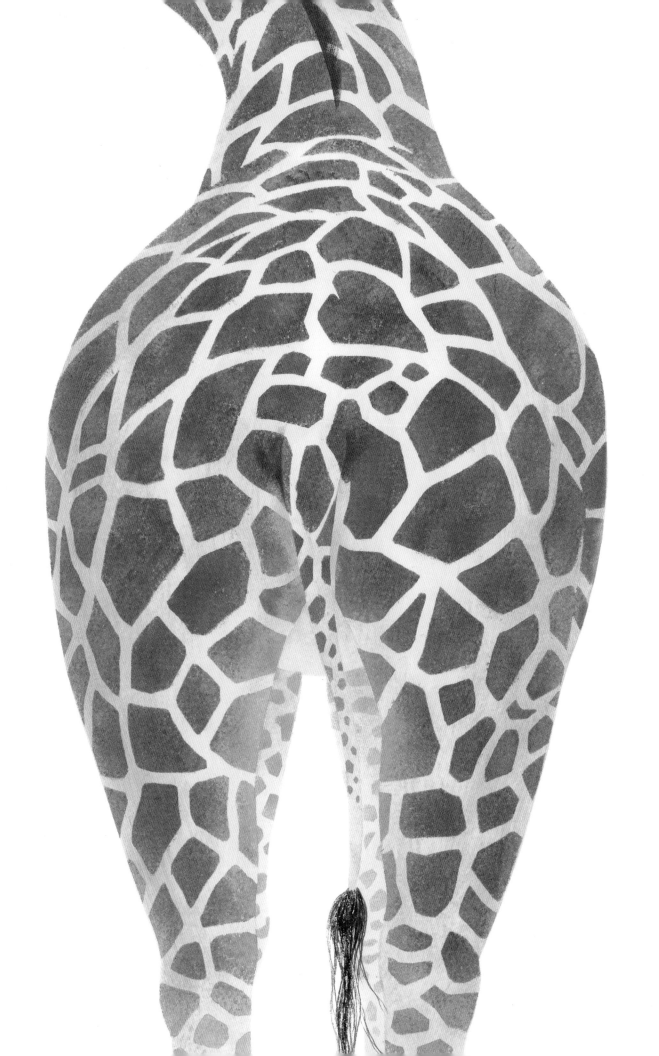

Our bottoms are **white,** **black,**

and black and white!

Our bottoms are the same color as our faces.

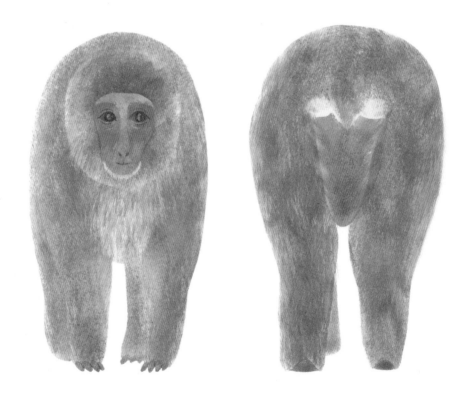

Did our faces copy our bottoms?

Or did our bottoms copy our faces?

Line up! Line up!

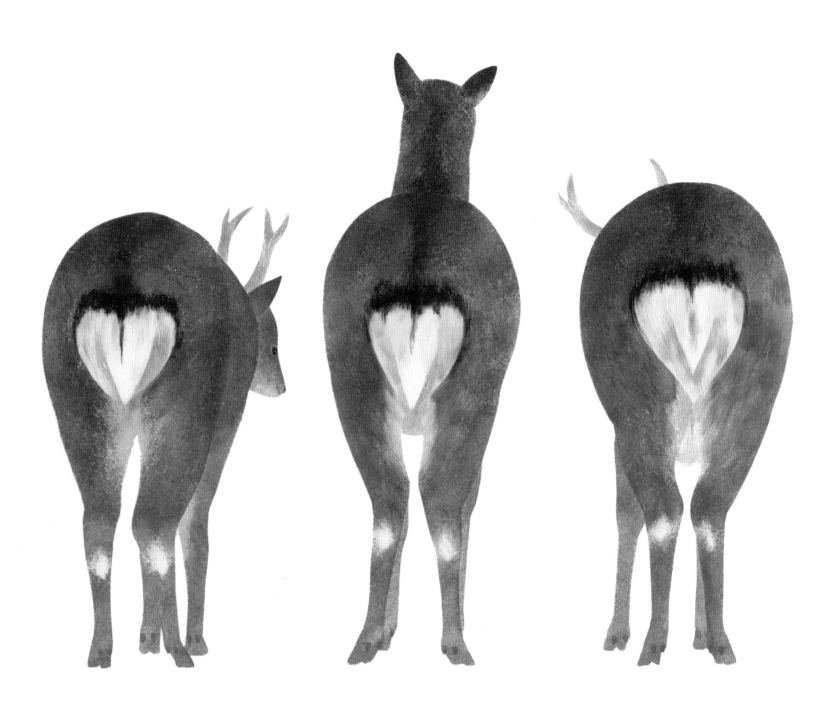

Heart-shaped bottoms, all in a row!

Our bottoms
are fluffy bottoms.

Even when it's cold,
we stay warm.

Our bottoms are tough bottoms.
When something bangs against them,
it doesn't bother us at all.

Our bottoms are spiky bottoms.
They're amazing too, don't you think?

Everyone's proud of their bottoms!

Such wonderful bottoms—each and every one!

MAKI SAITO is an artist and author known for her unique artistic methods using paper collage, stenciled paintings, and bingata, a traditional Japanese dyeing technique developed in Okinawa. She has written and illustrated several books in Japanese, inspired by her love for all living creatures in nature. *Animals Brag About Their Bottoms* is her first book in English. She lives in Tokyo, Japan.

ANIMALS IN THIS BOOK, IN ORDER OF APPEARANCE:

Rabbit, hippopotamus, Asian elephant, tiger, zebra, okapi, giraffe, polar bear, Asian black bear, panda, Malayan tapir, Japanese macaque, mandrill, deer, sheep, alpaca, armadillo, Indian rhinoceros, hedgehog, porcupine